The Ants go Marching!

illustrated by Dan Crisp

Child's Play (International) Ltd
Ashworth Rd, Bridgemead, Swindon SN5 7YD, UK

Swindon   Auburn ME   Sydney

ISBN 978-1-84643-618-5   L1408208X810206185

© 2007 Child's Play (International) Ltd   This edition © 2013

Printed in Heshan, China

5 7 9 10 8 6

www.childs-play.com

The ants go marching one by one, hurrah, hurrah!
The ants go marching one by one, hurrah, hurrah!
The ants go marching one by one,
The little one stops to suck his thumb,
And they all go marching down to the ground,
To get out of the rain... BOOM! BOOM! BOOM!

The ants go marching two by two, hurrah, hurrah!
The ants go marching two by two, hurrah, hurrah!
The ants go marching two by two,
The little one stops to tie his shoe,
And they all go marching down to the ground,
To get out of the rain … BOOM! BOOM! BOOM!

The ants go marching three by three, hurrah, hurrah!
The ants go marching three by three, hurrah, hurrah!
The ants go marching three by three,
The little one stops to climb a tree,
And they all go marching down to the ground,
To get out of the rain … BOOM! BOOM! BOOM!

The ants go marching four by four, hurrah, hurrah!
The ants go marching four by four, hurrah, hurrah!
The ants go marching four by four,
The little one stops to shut the door,
And they all go marching down to the ground,
To get out of the rain ... BOOM! BOOM! BOOM!

5x5

The ants go marching five by five, hurrah, hurrah!
The ants go marching five by five, hurrah, hurrah!
The ants go marching five by five,
The little one stops to take a dive,
And they all go marching down to the ground,
To get out of the rain ... BOOM! BOOM! BOOM!

The ants go marching six by six, hurrah, hurrah!
The ants go marching six by six, hurrah, hurrah!
The ants go marching six by six,
The little one stops to pick up sticks,
And they all go marching down to the ground,
To get out of the rain ... BOOM! BOOM! BOOM!

The ants go marching seven by seven,
Hurrah, hurrah!
The ants go marching seven by seven,
Hurrah, hurrah!
The ants go marching seven by seven,
The little one stops to count to eleven,
And they all go marching
Down to the ground,
To get out of the rain …

BOOM! BOOM! BOOM!

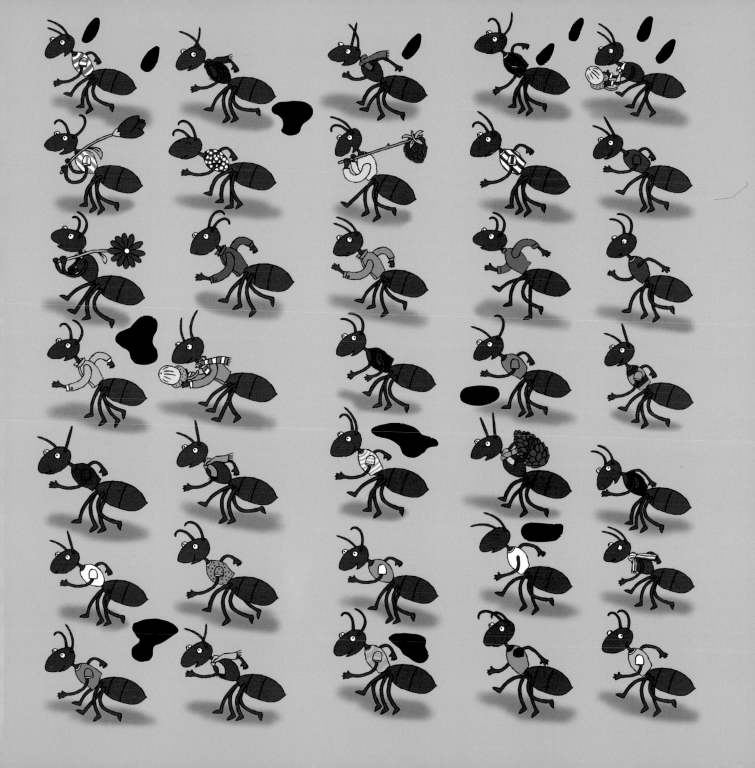

The ants go marching eight by eight,
Hurrah, hurrah!
The ants go marching eight by eight,
Hurrah, hurrah!
The ants go marching eight by eight,
The little one stops to shut the gate,
And they all go marching
Down to the ground,
To get out of the rain...

BOOM! BOOM! BOOM!

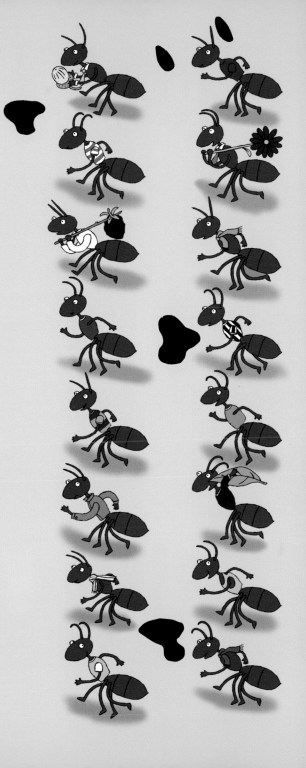

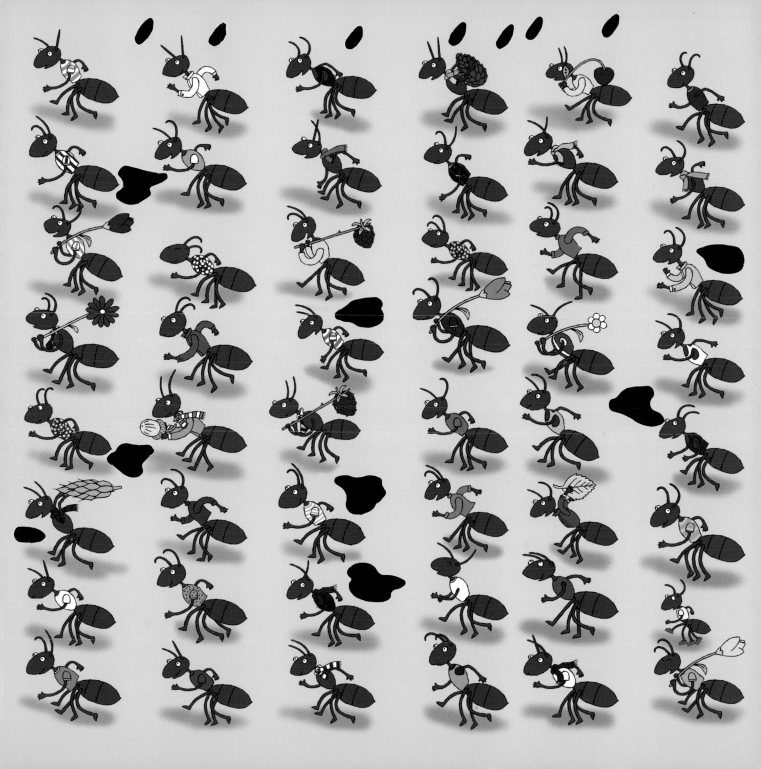

The ants go marching nine by nine,
Hurrah, hurrah!
The ants go marching nine by nine,
Hurrah, hurrah!
The ants go marching nine by nine,
The little one stops to check the time,
And they all go marching
Down to the ground,
To get out of the rain …

BOOM! BOOM! BOOM!

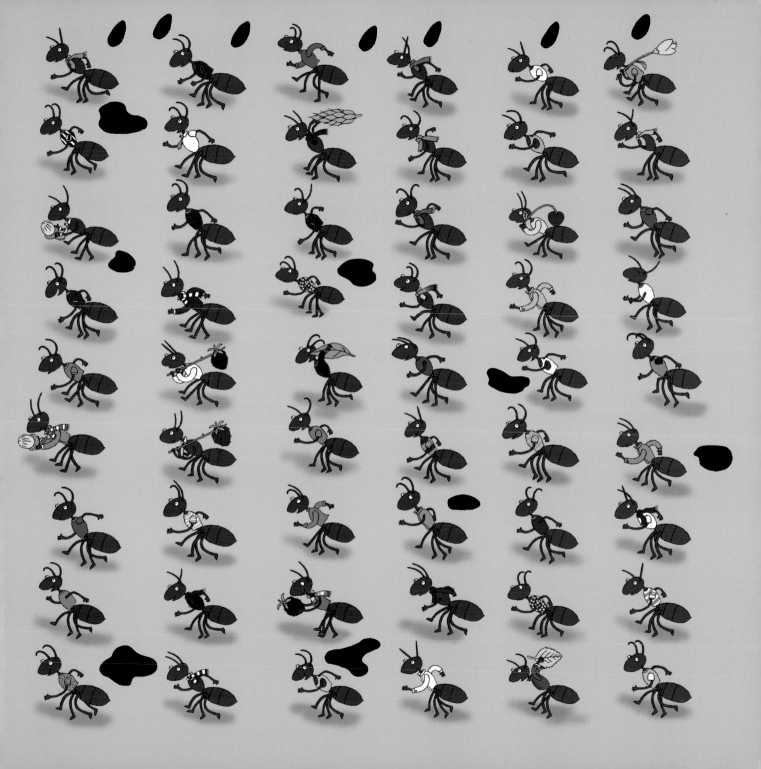

The ants go marching ten by ten,
Hurrah, hurrah!
The ants go marching ten by ten,
Hurrah, hurrah!
The ants go marching ten by ten,
The little one stops to say "THE END!"
And they all go marching
Down to the ground,
To get out of the rain...

BOOM! BOOM! BOOM!

The End!

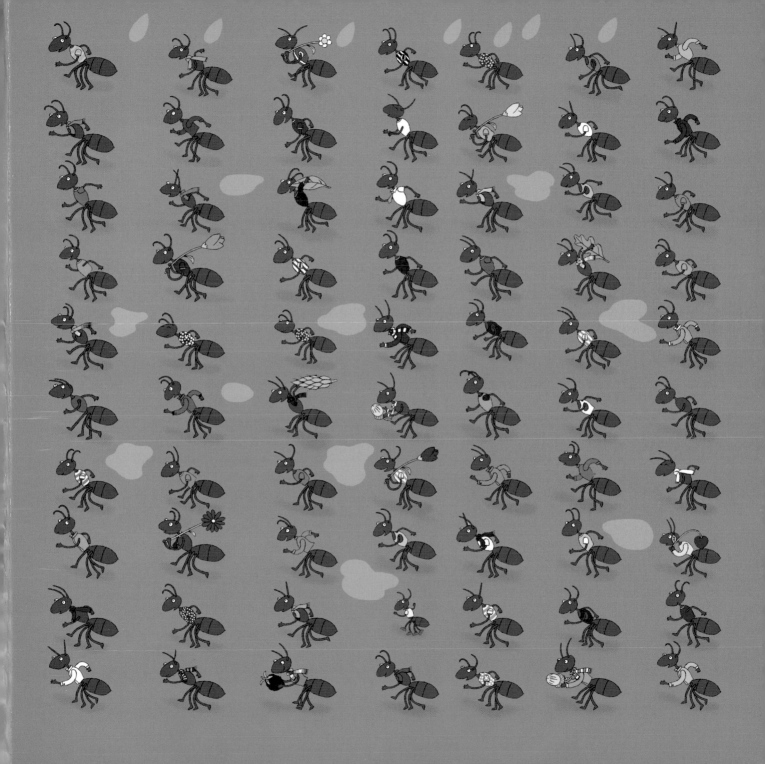

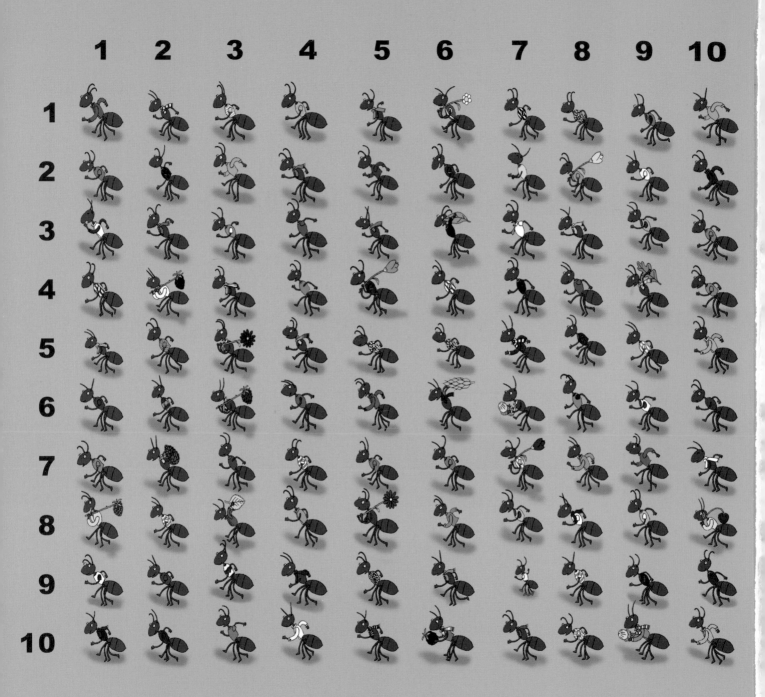